Puffin Books

WOULDN'T YOU LIKE TO K

This is a book for anyone who thinks poetry is soppy and all about daffodils and moonlight. It isn't always. In the hands of Michael Rosen it can be about big brothers and little sisters; dogs called Jim and Sid; places like Oldham, Newham, Upshot and Caughtshort. In fact, about the incidents, excitements and *bothers* we all experience.

Michael Rosen has written nine new poems especially for this Puffin paperback edition of *Wouldn't You Like to Know* – this is the first time they've appeared in a book. And among them is a great new encounter down behind the dustbin with the dog Sid!

A ten- or eleven-year-old will probably enjoy this book most . . . but there's lots in it for older children too.

WOULDN'T YOU LIKE TO KNOW

Down behind the dustbin
I met a dog called Joe.
'What have you got there?' I said.
'Wouldn't you like to know!'

Words by Michael Rosen

Pictures by Quentin Blake

PUFFIN BOOKS

Puffin Books, Penguin Books Ltd, Harmondsworth, Middlesex, England
Penguin Books, 625 Madison Avenue, New York, New York 10022, U.S.A.
Penguin Books Australia Ltd, Ringwood, Victoria, Australia
Penguin Books Canada Ltd, 2801 John Street, Markham, Ontario, Canada L3R 1B4
Penguin Books (N.Z.) Ltd, 182–190 Wairau Road, Auckland 10, New Zealand

First published by André Deutsch 1977
This edition, with new poems (pages 7–12, 30 and 92–3), published in Puffin Books 1981

Made and printed in Great Britain by
Richard Clay (The Chaucer Press) Ltd, Bungay, Suffolk
Set in Monotype Garamond

Contents

Contents *continued*

IMPORTANT MESSAGE

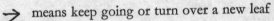

✱ means start

→ means keep going or turn over a new leaf

* Here is the News from space

The Space News Agency Atmos report
that the sun can be seen quite a lot
these days,
but not very much
at night.

The spokesman in the moon said:
'Hey diddle diddle
the cat and the fiddle
the cow jumped over the moon.
The little dog laughed
to see such fun
and the dish ran away with the spoon.'

Venus police have issued identikit pictures
of the cat and the cow, and
a dish is being held for questioning.
Police have put out a special appeal
for any little dog at or near the moon
at the time
to come forward and help with further investigation
of the affair.

Words in space

✳ They decided to abolish the words:
to sit
to stand
and to lie
and the word
to float will replace them.

So people now say:
float up straight when I'm talking to you
let sleeping dogs float
let's float down and have a chat about it.

People who don't like cabbage say,
I can't float cabbage
and they watch telly
in the floating-room.

Is there anyone who doesn't
underfloat what I'm saying?

I

End of the road on Earth

 'Last stop
everybody out
we turn round here you know.
Come on
everybody off
this is as far as we go.'

II

End of the road in space

'We're here?'
'Where?'
'You know.'
'No.'
'On a . . . in a . . . place.'
'But . . . this is a nowhere place.'
'This is the nowhere they call space.'

Loach

✳ The best pet I ever had
was a fish I caught in a net.
It was three inches long
and it had six whiskers round its mouth.
I looked it up in a book
and they said it was called a loach,
not roach – loach.

I put it in a tank
but the tank was by the window
where the sun came in,
so the tank went green,
a very very dark green
And no one believed
I had anything in there –
let alone anything called a loach.

Sometimes I'd go and sit by the tank,
and look in.
And I wouldn't see anything at all.
And sometimes I'd go and sit by the tank
and the loach would suddenly
come to the wall of the tank
where I could see it,
and I'd watch it
push the glass wall
push its whiskers along the gravel on the bottom
and then go back into the dark green water
where I couldn't see it, any more.

But no one believed I had anything in there
because no one ever sat by the tank
long enough to see it.

Small people's bus queue song

* We stand in the queue
for ages and ages
until our bus comes along.
Then everyone makes a dash for it
and we can never get on.

Look, here it comes –
it'll happen all over again.
We make a dash for it
and we're left out in the rain.

✳ I got on a bus to go shopping
and I saw
and I heard
'Green tomato chutney'
'Fresh cottage cheese'
'Shop-Along Bingo'
'All fares please'

ME: I went out and looked about
and saw a broken pram.

YOU: I went out and looked about
and saw the derby ram.

ME: For sale in the market:
a broken pram on broken wheels,
hot dogs and jellied eels,
a blue car with parking lights
but nowhere free to park it.

YOU: In a field on a farm:
the derby ram and all his sheep,
two cows fast asleep
and swallows swooping in and out
the shadows in the barn.

BOTH: We went out and looked about.
We went walking round.

YOU: I went up the country.
ME: I went down the town.

✳ My uncle Ronnie
took me to Hackney Downs
and said:
how's your eyes?
how far can you see with your eyes?

so I said:
I can see that tree over there.
so he said:
aha. But can you see the leaves on the tree over
    there?
and I said:
I can see that tree
I can see the leaves
on that tree over there.

All right, he says,
you say you can see the leaves on that tree.
Now, Mick, I'm telling you true
I can see a fly
sitting on a leaf
in that tree.
How about you?   →

and I said:
I don't know.
I'm not sure.
Perhaps.
Maybe.
Sort of.
Nearly.

Now, says my uncle Ron,
you see that tree
you see those leaves
you see that fly
well I tell you
I can see a leg
on that fly
on the leaf
on that tree over there
and what's more –
I can see a hair
on the leg of that fly
on the leaf on that tree over there
and –

Ronnie, I said, Uncle Ron
I can't see the hair on the leg
Uncle Ron, *I* can't see where the hair is.

The hair's on the knee, Mick,
the hair's on the knee.
Quick, look. Just there, quick.
Oh bad luck. You're too late.
The feller's gone and gone.

* The man on the corner
with broken glasses
sits on the bench
and watches who passes.

✳ My brother gets letters – not many, but some,
I don't know why – but I get none.
Odd people seem to write to him –
a card to say his bike's done or a library book's in.
He seems to have friends, who when they're away
write about their holiday,
like – 'We're near the beach, – had chips last night,
my bed squeaks and sand fleas bite.'
And sometimes he gets letters out of the blue
from people who can't know who they're writing to
offering him *The Reader's Digest Bird Book* cheap
or adverts for films like 'The Blobs' – GIANT
    JELLIES THAT EAT AS THEY CREEP.
But I don't get anything. No one writes to me.
That is – until just recently.

You see I was looking at the paper one day
and I was reading about this man's brain – it was
    fading away.
That is – until he had done this 'Memory Course'
and discovered his Inner Mind Force.
And when you got down to the end
It said: 'This sounds GREAT – please send
to me at this address now:
"SO YOU WANT TO SAVE BRAIN-CELLS? –
    HERE'S HOW".'
And you filled in your name and address along
    dotted lines
and sent it off to: 'Great Minds
P.O. Box 16, Manchester 8.'
It was as simple as that. Sit and wait.

→

Now as it happens I wasn't very worried about my
   Inner Mind Force
or the ones to cure baldness or put me on a
   slimming course,
but the thing was – they all had something for free
which they promised they'd send – addressed to me.
What could be better?
I'd get a letter.
So after I'd got some of these forms together
I came back then to my brother
and I said: 'I bet, out of us two,
I get more letters than you.'
And he said: 'Rubbish, no one ever writes to you,
you're a Nobody, a No-one-knows-who.'
'Right,' I said, 'we'll keep a score,
me and you – see who gets more.'
'Great,' he said, and shook my hand. 'Done!
What do I get,' he said, 'when I've won?'
'No prizes,' I said. 'But whoever loses,
will have to do whatever the winner chooses.'

→

'Great,' he said again – and laughed,
he must have thought I was daft
to take him on.
He thought he couldn't go wrong.
'I'll show him,' I thought. 'What I can't wait to see
is his face when these people write back to me.'

So anyway, I sent off about three or four
and soon I got what I was hoping for.
A former Mr Universe had written to say:
'BUILD POWER-PACKED MUSCLES
in just 70 seconds a day!!!'
'There you are,' I said to my brother.
'A letter – One nil – and tomorrow I'll be getting
    another.'
So while he read what they had sent me
'Rippling muscles on guarantee
see your strength rise
right before your very eyes
on the built-in POWER-METER,'
I sat tight for my next letter.

→

Next to come through the post was Harvey Speke.
'I see my years of fatness as a past nightmare I'll
   never repeat.
Why be fat when you can be slim?
Shrink your waistline, stomach and chin,
I used to look like THIS – believe it or not!'
And there were pictures of bellies and heaven knows
   what
before and after shrinking with the Miracle Pill.
I didn't read the rest – 'Two nil!'
I said to my brother. 'I'm winning, aren't I?
You can't win now.' But he says: 'Oh can't I?'
and I can see he's getting really angry
reading about pills to stop you feeling hungry.

Next day there were two more –
one was a rather glossy brochure
on an Old Age Pension Plan
and the other on Shoes For The Larger Man.
For three days he hadn't got anything through the
   post.
He sat there at breakfast munching his toast
staring at his plate while I was making a neat stack
of leaflets and letters I'd got back. →

'Four nil now, isn't it? Give in?
You see,' I said, 'every day I'm getting something.'
And sure enough *something* arrived not long after
but it wasn't quite what *I* was after.

It was a great big parcel – it had come from
   Liverpool.
'Who's it for?' I said. 'You, you fool.'
It was the first parcel I'd ever had in my life.
'Go on – open it,' father said, 'here's a knife.'
And they all stood round to see who'd sent a parcel
   to me.
Even my brother wanted to see.
It was wrapped in red paper but the box was brown.
I pulled the lid off – and it was an eiderdown.
It was what is nowadays called a Quilt for a bed,
But we used to call them 'eiderdowns', instead.
'What is it?' 'A pillow?'
'Who sent it?' 'I don't know.'
'How much did it cost you?' 'What do you mean?'
'Don't be funny – he hasn't got a bean.'
I panicked. I came over cold.
Don't forget – I was only nine years old.
'Did you send off for this thing?'
'No,' I said. 'All I did was fill a form thing in,
it said there was something for free –
fill in the form and it'd come to me.'
'Fat-head! That means free till the seventh day,
keep it longer than that and you've got to pay.
Send it back if you don't.
Mind you – I bet you won't.'
'Don't say that,' said mother, 'he wasn't to know
   better.'
'But what was he doing?' 'I wanted a letter.'
'Well get your friend Mart to send you cards from
   Wales when he goes
instead of sending off for boxes of bed-clothes.'

→

23

I felt such an idiot looking at the eiderdown.
I looked at my brother. He looked round.
'What's the matter? Five nil. Well done.'
He laughed. 'I think you've won
or do you want to go on for a bit more?'
'No no no,' I said, 'I don't care about the score.'
'So you'll wrap up the box and send it back?' father
    said.
'Unless you want to pay for a new eiderdown on
    your bed.'
But I didn't do it straightaway,
and I didn't do it the next day,
or the next, or the next,
the eiderdown and the wrapping were in a gigantic
    mess.

→

'The eiderdown's growing,' I was thinking,
'No! The box to send it back in's shrinking.'
Anyway fourth day on – eiderdown still not sent
we were all having tea – the doorbell went.

My brother looks up. 'Probably the police –
on the hunt for an eiderdown thief.'
Father went to see who was there
and we could hear voices from where we were.
Moment later – he's back – very long in the face,
he looks at me. 'It's for you,' he says.
I could have died. 'Is it the police
on the hunt for an eiderdown thief?'
'No,' he says, there's a man out there.
He's got something for you.' 'Out where?
Men don't come round here for me.'
But I went to the door and they all followed to see. →

'Mr Rosen, is it?' The man looked.
He was reading my name out of a black book.
'No,' I said. 'You want my father.'
'*M*. Rosen?' he says. 'He's *H*, I gather.'
I said, 'Yes. I'm M.'
So he says, 'Good. Right then,
it's outside. Shall I wheel it in?'
'What?' I said. 'The washing machine.'
'Washing machine? Oh no. Not for me.'
'Well it says here "*M*. Rosen", all right. Do you want
    to see?'
'No,' I said, 'I only send for free things.'
'Yes, the demonstrations *are* free,' he says, 'but not
    the washing machines.'
'I don't want it.' I looked round for help.
You can imagine how I felt.
But they were hiding behind the door
laughing their heads off – my brother on the floor.
I turned back. Looked up at the man.
'I've brought it now,' he says. 'It's in the van.'
'I've come all the way from Hoover's to show it
    you.'
'No,' I said. 'No?' he said. 'Haven't you got anyone
    else I could show it to?'
For a moment – it felt like a week –
he looked down at me – I looked down at my feet.
Then he shut his book and went, and I shut the door,
and straightaway my brother was there with 'Shall I
    add that to your score?

→

Six nil? Have you won yet?'
I said, 'I've had enough of this letter bet.'
And he said, 'Why? Don't you want a washing
   machine?
You could use it to keep your eiderdown clean!'
'Oh no! The eiderdown.' For a moment I'd
   forgotten about it.
'I can't get it in. The box: – it's shrunk!' I shouted.
But mum said, 'I'll help you send that back, don't
   worry,
but what's coming next? A coat? A lorry?'
But father said, 'Who's won this bet?
And what's the winner going to get?'
My brother looked really happy and said, 'I've lost –
Letters? *He's* the one that gets the most.'
'All I want,' I said, 'is I don't want to hear any
   more about it.
If I have to send off to get a letter – I'm better off
   without it.'
'OK,' my brother said, 'let's call it square.'
'Yes,' I said, 'we'll leave it there.'

But even now –
when there's someone asking for me at the door,
who mum has never seen before,
she says to me: 'It's for you, dear.
Quick! Your eiderdown's here!'

✳ Down behind the dustbin
I met a dog called Sid.
He could smell a bone inside
but couldn't lift the lid.

 ✳ Down behind the dustbin
I met a dog called Jim.
He didn't know me
and I didn't know him.

 ✳ Down behind the dustbin
I met a dog called Sid.
He said he didn't know me,
but I'm pretty sure he did.

✳ Made a boat
from sticks and cloth –
put it on the water
to see it float.

Go boat, go boat
sail across that sea
go boat
and sail on back to me.

It's sea and sky all the way over
my boat flies out across the water
but always comes on back to me.

It's a good boat
go boat
she's a sail boat
my boat.

Go boat, go boat
sail across that sea
go boat
and sail on back to me.

❋ I'm the youngest in our house
so it goes like this:

My brother comes in and says:
'Tell him to clear the fluff
out from under his bed.'
Mum says,
'Clear the fluff
out from under your bed.'
Father says,
'You heard what your mother said.'
'What?' I say.
'The fluff,' he says.
'Clear the fluff
out from under your bed.'
So I say,
'There's fluff under his bed, too,
you know.'
So father says,
'But we're talking about the fluff
under *your* bed.'
'You will clear it up
won't you?' mum says.
So now my brother – all puffed up –
says,
'Clear the fluff
out from under your bed,
clear the fluff
out from under your bed.'
Now I'm angry. I am angry.
So I say – what shall I say?
I say,
'Shuttup Stinks
YOU CAN'T RULE MY LIFE.'

✳ Mum'll be coming home today.
It's three weeks she's been away.
When dad's alone
all we eat
is cold meat
which I don't like
and he burns the toast I want just-brown
and I hate taking the ash-can down.

He's mended the door
from the little fight
on Thursday night
so it doesn't show
and can we have grilled tomatoes
Spanish onions and roast potatoes
and will you sing me 'I'll never more roam'
when I'm in bed, when you've come home?

Mum's reply

If you like your toast
done just-brown
then take it out
before it burns.
You hate taking the ash-can down?
Well now you know
what I know
so we might as well take turns.

But now I'm back,
yes let's have grilled tomatoes
Spanish onions and roast potatoes
because you know
when I was away
I wanted nothing more
than be back here
and see you all.

* Late last night
I lay in bed
driving buses
in my head.

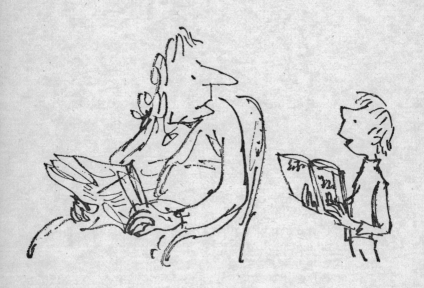

* ME: 'Late last night
I lay in bed.'

GRAN: 'You lay in lead?'
ME: '"In bed," I said'

GRAN: 'You led your bed?'
ME: 'I said: "I lay"'

GRAN: 'You lay in bed?
You should have said.'

✳ One evening in the bay of Lipari
on rocks that look over the harbour water
a man sits with his chin stuck into his shoulder
fishing for rainbow fish
with a long green rod and line.

Crouching in the pools behind him
we collect the rainbows in a beer crate
watching on that line.
The float dips. The man doesn't move.
We flick water across the fish to keep them fresh,
the sun still stands against the tower
and its shadow falls across the water.

Then the rod whips, up flies the float –
but nothing more. Thirteen rainbows, it stays.
We watch him roll a roll of bread in his mouth
to bait his hook again
and we duck
as past our ears go bread hook and float
all on the end of the long rod and line.

Thirteen rainbows out of the sea.
It can't be bad. Fourteen would be better.
More fish; more soup. There's five middling,
five tiddlers and three whoppers.
Or if you stack them up the other way
three whoppers, five middling, five tiddlers.
We have a line too, because under these rocks
live moray eels.

→

Yards and yards of eel, writhing about
just where the round the edge
where the over the through the under
where there here, where we lower our hook
with a lump of raw rainbow dangling.

No sooner said
when yes he'd slid out
and taken the bait. He's got it.
We've got it. He takes the bait
he takes the hook. He takes the hook
he takes the line – he'll have your fingers too.

Let go pull him
he pulls, pull him, I said. The line breaks,
and without a turn about or round about
he's in reverse and slides back along his tracks
to where it is his tracks backtrack to.

The sun sets behind the tower.
Three whoppers, five middling and five or
four or five . . . Four tiddlers –
Can't be bad.

The man's float still rises and falls.
He knows there's more where they came from.
He can feel them nibbling down there.
You can almost see them cruising
in a complete quiet
in the last rays of the day

→

the line dropping out of the light above
down to where they nudge about very cool
gliding round this right little chunk
of sweet nibble lump thing
that breaks off crumbs in the current
if you can bear to wait
if they can wait.
We wait.
One can't.
The whole lump he takes. The lot.
And up, up out of the quiet
into the sky like a silver bird
wey op wey op wey op
he's on the line
his last moment is a ride in the sky
wild, he flies on air with his fins
he must fall
and down he swings
once fast past the man's hand
once slap into it.
He holds that fish's wriggle alright
and takes his hook back
flings it to us on the rocks.

There's still life.
There's still heart and blood
the fins still stretch for the water.
He flips so strong
it could carry him to Spain and back –
underwater.
Here it turns him over and over
somersaulter
he keeps flipping.
Perhaps he can feel the smell of water
only inches away.
He keeps flipping for that water.
He could make it.

→

If we didn't like fish-soup
he could really make it.
We're on to him,
get our fingers round his belly
slide them down to that flashy tail
and crack his head against the rock.
Crack it again number fourteen
crack it once more and put him down.
Lie him down in the old beer crate.
He's middling.
Three whoppers, four tiddlers, six middlers.
Thirteen. Thirteen? I thought –
The old thirteen is being minced with line and hook
in a cold black crack by the moray eel
in the rocks somewhere.
Time for us to go.

As we leave, climbing over the rocks
back to the road,
the man looks out across the harbour
and near across a rubbish tip
where all the pots bottles boxes and crates in the
    world
have come.
He looks up the cliff above the tip
to the hotel that empties and drops the pots
and spits.

We'll have soup
so long as we've got fish.
Come on.

✳ Your brother Danny's got a golden nose
and fish swim out of his eyes.
Your brother Danny's got legs like rhubarb
and ears like apple pies.

✳ I'm just going out for a moment.

Why?

To make a cup of tea.

Why?

Because I'm thirsty.

Why?

Because it's hot.

Why?

Because the sun's shining.

Why?

Because it's summer.

Why?

Because that's when it is.

Why?

Why don't you stop saying why?

Why?

Tea-time. That's why.
High-time-you-stopped-saying-why-time.

What?

The train now standing
at Flatworm's heaven
will not stop or start
at Oldham, Newham
You bring 'em, We buy 'em,
and all stations to
Kahalacahoo, Hawaii.

All messengers for
Upshot, Caughtshort
Stick 'em up and Hijack
should travel in the slow coaches
at the rear of the train.

All passengers with messages
for Uncle Harry's cabbages
should stake their seats
in quicker coaches
now that Uncle Harry's cabbages
need weeding out
and watering.

I am a wasp.
I am stuck in a sticky jar
I used to fly in the wind
buzz my wings in the sun
and hover in sweet places

but I am stuck in a sticky jar.

Up I fly
and my wings hit a tin lid
my hard yellow head knocks it
so down I glide for a flicker of a second
and my legs, my body
are in sweet water where there is no breath to
    breathe.

I used to soar and swoop
I used to circle round and round
and settle on sweet things

but I am stuck in a sticky jar.

Above me the heat of the sun
pours through holes in the tin.
I buzz and crawl to them.
Isn't that the way I came in?
– but nearly there, my feelers
hit tin.
The ragged cut edge of tin.
And who am I to dare to drag this weak waist
across that edge?

→

Beneath me, all about me,
is the smell of crushed strawberry.
It doesn't grow stronger if I buzz nearer.
It doesn't grow weak if I hover or move.
It's strong everywhere in smell
and nowhere to be found.

I used to *find* crushed strawberries –
or maybe melting chocolate, the hearts of fat plums.
I used to cut my way to the syrup of bruised bananas
in the gutters of the market.
I used to linger on the rims of glasses and bottles
to nibble at the crystals of lemonade, cherryade
and old orange pop.

All around me now
other wasps, even a bee and a blue-bottle
buzz up buzz down
and we're all swerving to miss each other's wings.

I turn back.
One is at my foot.
I twist to dodge him
but he is at my neck.
I snip at his scales –
he twists, a hairsbreadth from my eye.
A sting sticks, waves to find
a soft spot to get in.
I cut back, take off
and my wing is flying in the sweet water
dragging me down.

→

I use my legs and run up over the backs
of wasps floating where water and glass meet.
They sink. I sink.
And the buzz in the sweet smell of the air
goes on and on.
There is heat in the sun through the holes
in the lid of the tin.
The heat pours in.
Up above me, my eyes shadowy with the sugar
see a hole for the heat.

Into it come the eyes, the feelers, the jaws,
the head, the legs, the chest, the –

Those of us in here could say:
Go back.

But those of us in here who could say
are no more than black and yellow scum,
dead froth bobbing on the water.

In through the hole comes the chest,
the wings, the waist, the body and the sting.

Too late,
you silly, sugar-sniffing, soft nibbling, sweet-sucker.
That's the end.

* The angry hens from Never-when
had a fight and lost their legs.
Now it's hot
where they squat
and they're laying soft-boiled eggs.

57

* I went to the doctor, yes,
I went to him
and I said – 'Doctor, Doctor,
it's Roads,' I said. 'Roads?' he says.
'Roads,' I said.
'No such thing,' he says.
'I've got Roads, Doctor,
very bad Roads.
I've got long distance lorryworry
one way only lorryworry.
They say:
No U-turns Ahead.
I know I turned my head,
but I saw 2 zebras crossing
and a bus eating traffic jam.
I can hear
unhappy new gears.

→

When traffic's light
at traffic lights
I see red
amber
red and amber
red already.
I wish I was a
windscreen wiper.
Once I washed windscreens
now I watch wipers.
What shall I do?
I've got Roads,
very bad Roads, Doctor.
What shall I do?'

So he looked at me and said:
'I don't know what I know
but I've got just the stink for you.'
and he squeezed me on the Underground
and handed me the tube.

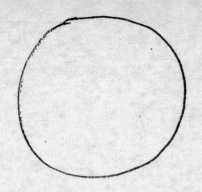

In an old book called
The Travels of Sir John Mandeville
there is a story of an amazing bird called

THE PHOENIX

On the banks of the Nile
lies the city of Heliopolis
the city of the sun

And in that city is a place of stone
paved flat and round like a ring.

→

There, one morning
when the end of time will come
they'll spread live sulphur on the ground
and spices brought from the hills.

The sun will rise, the people will cry
a spark will fall, a flame will rise
out of the sky will fly the Phoenix bird
with a crest of feathers upon his head
his beak as blue as the Indian sea.

With his wings spread like an eagle
and tail spread like a fan
into the fire he will fly
to burn among the spices
for a day and a night through.   →

There on the stones in the ring
as night turns into day
and the sun fills the sky,
there amongst the ashes
men shall look and find a worm.

On the second day next after,
that worm will become Phoenix alive
after the night of fire
and on the third
the Phoenix bird will take its ashes up
from the place of fire
and fly with every bird from every bush
back to the sun in the sky.

That is the story of the Phoenix bird
who lives alone in the sun
and dies where he is born.

Think of this tower-block
as if it was a street standing up
and instead of toing and froing
in buses and cars
you up and down it
in a high speed lift.

There will be no pavement artists of course
because there aren't any pavements.
There isn't room for a market
but then there isn't room for cars.
No cars: no accidents
but don't lean
out of the windows
don't play in the lifts
or they won't work.
They don't work
and they won't work
if you play Split Kipper,
Fox and Chickens, Dittyback,
Keek-bogle, Jackerback,
Huckey-buck, Hotchie-pig,
Foggy-plonks, Ching Chang Cholly
or Bunky-Bean Bam-Bye.

→

Go down. The stairs are outside –
you can't miss them – try not to miss them, please.
No pets.
Think how unhappy they'd be
locked in a tower-block.
There will be
no buskers, no hawkers
no flowers, no chinwaggers
no sandwich boards,
no passers-by,
except for
low-flying aircraft
or high-flying sparrows.

Here is a note from Head Office:
you will love your neighbour
left right above below
so no music, creaky boots,
caterwauling somersaulting –
never never never jump up or down
or you may
never never never get down or up again.
No questions.
It's best to tip-toe,
creep, crawl, and whisper.
If there *are* any
problems phone me
and I'll be out.
Good day.

✳ I put out to sea
   in a wooden row-boat
   with a cheese and pickle sandwich
   and a yellow hat and coat.

✳ Ask no questions
tell no lies.
Ever seen mincemeat
in mince pies?

From a problem page

✳ Dear Maureen,
I am a lamp-post.
Every Saturday evening at five o'clock
three boys
wearing blue and white scarves
blue and white hats
waving their arms in the air
and shouting,
come my way.
Sometimes they kick me.
Sometimes they kiss me.
What should I do
to get them to make up their minds?
Yours bewilderedly,
Annie Onlight.

✳ Here is the News:

In Manchester today a man was seen
with hair on top of his head.
Over now straightway to our Northern
    correspondent:
Hugh Snews.

→

'It's been a really incredible day
here in Manchester. Scenes like this
have been seen here everyday
for years and years. It's now quite certain
no one will be saying anything about this
for months to come. One eyewitness said so.
"Are you sure?" I said.
She said: "No."
Back to you in London.'

All round the world,
newspapers, radio and television
have taken no notice of this story
and already a Prime Minister
has said nothing about it at all.
What next?
Rumour McRumourbungle,
Expert expert in expert experts?

'I doubt it. I doubt whether
anyone *will* doubt it – but I do.'

'What?'

'Doubt it.'

Thank you, Rumour McRumourbungle.
But how did it all begin?
As dawn broke in Manchester it soon became clear.
It's quite likely there was a lot of air in the air.
An hour after a few minutes had gone,
a couple of seconds passed
and a minute later at 12.15
it was a quarter past twelve.

→

Suddenly from across the other side of the road,
on the side facing this side,
there was the same road from the other side.
This side was now facing that side
and the road on that other side
was still opposite this.
Then – it happened.
There is no question of this.
In fact – no one has questioned it at all.
Further proof of this comes from the police
who say that a woman held for questioning
was released immediately
because she didn't know the answers
to the questions that no one asked her . . .

So –
it's something of a mystery.
Yes –
it's a mysterious thing to some
and there are some who think
it could
in a mysterious way
be nothing at all.

Today was not
very warm
not very cold
not very dry
not very wet.

No one round here
went to the moon
or launched a ship
or danced in the street.

No one won a great race
or a big fight.

The crowds weren't out
the bands didn't play.

There were no flags no songs
no cakes no drums.
I didn't see any processions.
No one gave a speech.

Everyone thought today was ordinary,
busy busy
in out in
hum drummer day
dinner hurry
grind away day.

→

Nobody knows that today
was the most special day
that has ever ever been.

Ranzo, Reuben Ranzo,
who a week and a year ago was gone
lost
straying starving
under a bus? in the canal?
(the fireman didn't know)
was here, back,
sitting on the step
with his old tongue lolling,
his old eyes blinking.

I tell you –
I was so happy
So happy I tell you
I could have grown a tail –
and wagged it.

✳ Tip-top tip-top
  tap a speckled egg.
  Once to put him in his cup
  and twice to crack his head.

✳ What's in your head
Jacky lad, Jacky lad
what's in your head
Jacky lad?
Steak and kidney pie
and a slice of mouldy bread
that's what's in my head
lovely Mary

No, now tell me true
what's in your head, Jacky lad?
It is the thought of you
that's running in my head
but I didn't want to say
lovely Mary

I'm glad that you did
Jacky lad, Jacky lad
I'm glad that you did.
It'll keep me warm
when you're gone
Jacky lad, Jacky lad.
It'll keep me warm
when you're gone
Jacky lad.

Billy Silk looked at the sky:
'I tell you – it'll rain tonight.'
And when Billy Silk looks at the sky
he's nearly always right.

We went out at five
there wasn't a cloud in sight.
'Mark my words,' said Billy Silk.
'It's going to rain tonight.'

The lights were lit down Boatman's Walk
when we went to bed at nine.
You could have walked across that sea
on an alley of moonshine

And now before sunrise
we're at our windows again.
Billy hadn't lied you know:
the air was full of rain.

The roof is like a herring's sides
every tile is a scale
the chimneys stand like herring's fins
the gable as its tail.

The moon runs down Boatman's Walk
like water on a knife
and Billy Silk's at sea
where he's been all his life.

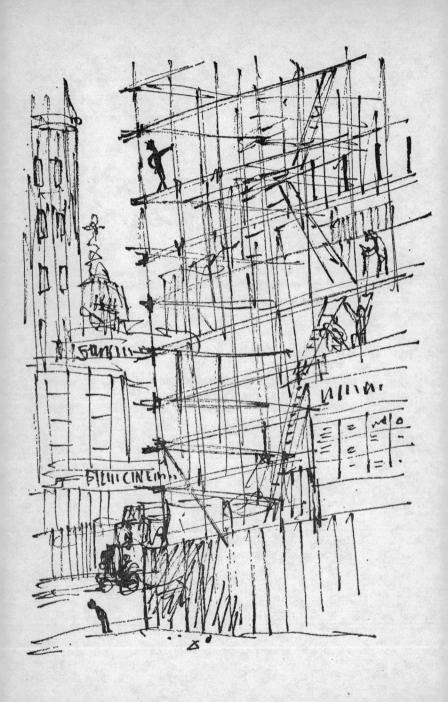

✳ Look – said the boy
the scaffold-man at work
is like a spider on his net

No – said the scaffold-man
I'm just a fly
in the trap the spider set

* The two-headed two-body,
the Demon Manchanda
had eyes bigger than his belly.
He walked and talked
right round the world
but every time he opened his mouth
he put his foot in it.

'You're pulling my leg,'
he said to himself.
So he ate his words instead.
I suppose you know the rest:
he went to the window
and threw out his chest.

✳ There was a man who used to stay in our house
and he had a crazy way of shutting the door.
He wouldn't let go of the handle.
It took him ages to shut a door.
First he closed the door
and then ages later
he let go of the handle
and it clicked shut.
We used to laugh about it
and try and do it just like him.
He'd be having breakfast with us
and my brother would get up to go out,
leaving me there with the man
and when it came for my brother to shut the door
behind him –
first he'd close the door,
and then ages later, my brother
he'd be outside the door
still hanging on to the handle.

→

Then all of a sudden he'd let go – and
it clicked shut,
and I'd hear him outside the door stuffing his hands
    into his mouth
to try and stop himself dying of laughter.
Meanwhile I was inside – alone with the man
trying to stop myself exploding too.

Once we were all having breakfast together
all our family – and him
and I said to him –
in front of everyone else:
'Hey you know, it's dead funny the way you shut the
    door.
Last night we were trying to do it just like you –
seeing who could do it best.'
And then everyone went very quiet and looked at me.
After that my dad began to call me 'Blabbermouth'
or Blabber for short.

✳ Good Friday fair
comes once a year
to our town, to our town
and we go down
to see what's there
to see the fair:

the ping-pong for a goldfish bowl,
lucky dip at the wishing well
I wish you well, mum –
tunnel to hell, mum?
I'd rather father,
we'll helter-skelter.
Poke a pig for penny-a-poke?
hoop-la, sorry I spoke.

(Did anyone see what goes on in the tent
at the end of the street, where no one went?)

Roll up rolla penny
rolla penny rollup.
Tell your weight while you wait
Don't give me no, sir.
Have a go, sir.
We aim to please
You aim, too, please
Go on stop.
Ever heard popcorn pop?
Try the candy-floss balloon-seller
roundabout fortune-teller.

Tell me –
did anyone see what goes on in the tent
at the end of the road, where no one went?